MY HAMSTER IS A

GENIUS

DAVE LOWE

ILLUSTRATED BY THE BOY FITZ HAMMOND

Piccadilly
PRESS

First published in Great Britain in 2012 by
PICCADILLY PRESS

This edition published in 2018 by
PICCADILLY PRESS
80–81 Wimpole St, London W1G 9RE
www.piccadillypress.co.uk

A CIP catalogue record for this book is available
from the British Library.

ISBN: 978-1-84812-655-8
also available as an ebook

1

Printed and bound by Clays Ltd, St Ives Plc

MIX
Paper from
responsible sources
FSC® C018072

Piccadilly Press is an imprint of Bonnier Zaffre Ltd,
a Bonnier Publishing company
www.bonnierpublishing.com

To Stacey, Rebecca and Miri –
thanks for all the pencils.
And to Glenn – thanks for the help.

THE JINKS FAMILY
Me, Lucy, Mum, Dad and Stinky

Chapter 1

Never sticky-tape your little sister to her bed, even if she asks you to. I did, and my mum went absolutely bananas.

Mum has a long history of unusual punishments. Once, when she caught me giving my sister's Barbie doll a haircut, she sat me down and cut my hair in the same style.

And now, thanks to the sticky-taping incident, my mum has locked my TV and all my games in the shed, and announced she was buying me a pet.

'You're nine years old now, Ben,' she said firmly. 'That's old enough to be responsible. If you can show me that you can actually take care of something, then you'll get your things back.'

I was speechless. But everyone else had an opinion on what pet to get.

My dad wanted a greyhound, so he could win money on it at the track.

Lucy, my recently sticky-taped little sister, wanted a pony.

My mum wanted something that was really small and really quiet.

Me, I went straight to my room, made a list and presented it to my mum.

BEN'S POSSIBLE PETS

1. Aardvark

2. Monkey or chimp of some kind (not a baboon)

3. Bee

4. Husky dog (and a pair of rollerblades, so I don't have to walk to school any more)

5. Medium-sized octopus (and medium-sized swimming pool)

6. Hairy-nosed wombat

Mum folded the list and slipped it into her jeans pocket.

Then she went to the pet shop and came back with a hamster.

Later, the four of us were having dinner around the kitchen table. The newest family member was in its cage by the sink, watching us stuff our faces. It was small, brown and furry, and it looked incredibly boring.

'What about calling her "Chloe"?' said Lucy. (Chloe was the name of that day's best friend. My sister changed best friends as often as most people change their socks.)

'We can't call the hamster "Chloe",' my mum said, 'because it's a boy.'

'How do you know?' my dad asked.

'How do you think?'

My dad picked the hamster out of its cage and squinted down at it, holding it upside down in his palm and blowing gently on its belly fluff.

'It must be very small,' he said, chuckling and putting it back. 'His ding-a-ling.'

My mum sighed.

'I'm not sure that's acceptable table-talk, Derek,' she said, then added: 'What about "Rover"? *That's* a male name.'

'It's also a dog's name, Mum,' I told her.

'Plus,' my dad said, grinning and waggling his fork towards the hamster, 'he's stuck in that cage with only a little wheel to run around on. He'll hardly be doing much *roving*, will he?' Then he had an idea: 'What about calling him "Red Rum", like the racehorse?'

We all groaned. Everything was horses with

my dad, or greyhounds, or anything he could lose money on.

I clanked down my cutlery.

Everyone stared at me. Even the hamster.

'If he's *my* pet,' I said, 'and *I* have to look after him –'

'You certainly do,' my mum interrupted.

'– then can't I call him whatever I want?'

'Not fair,' Lucy complained. 'It's a punishment pet, remember?'

My mum looked at my dad, who shrugged, and then she thought about it some more.

'So, Ben,' she said eventually, 'what are you going to call him?'

I said the stupidest name I could possibly think of:

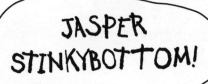

JASPER
STINKYBOTTOM!

Lucy giggled.

My dad rolled his eyes.

My mum frowned, shook her head for what seemed a really, really long time, and then let out a deep sigh.

But, as it turned out, there was someone who hated the name even more than my mum.

Chapter 2

I looked around my room for something – *anything* – to do. Normally I'd be watching TV, flicking through one of my old comics or shooting baddies on my PlayStation. Not tonight. Jasper Stinkybottom's cage was on the desk in front of me where all my fun stuff used to be, but my hamster was inside his little house and he was not budging.

My mum was in the living room, sewing a costume for Lucy's next show. My dad was next to her, watching the horse-racing on TV and struggling with a crossword.

My sister was practising tap-dancing in her room. The sound was really annoying – tappety-tap, tappety-tap – like someone was forever knocking on the door but never coming in.

And Jasper Stinkybottom, my very last hope for entertainment, seemed to be having a snooze.

I sighed. The situation was desperate: there was absolutely nothing to do except my homework.

And so, very reluctantly, I pulled my maths book from my schoolbag and stared at the first question.

I was already stumped. I scratched my head. I rubbed my chin. Finally, I read the question out loud, like I'd seen my dad do with his crossword clues (although it didn't seem to help him much).

'Eighty-five minus twenty-eight,' I said.

'Fifty-seven,' came a small, rough voice.

I glanced around. No one. I must have imagined it.

I said the sum once more, and again I heard a voice:

'That would be fifty-seven.'

It sounded like the whisper of someone with a bad cough.

I looked around, completely baffled. Was someone playing a joke on me? My sister wouldn't have known the answer, but it could have been my dad.

I got up, opened my bedroom door and looked around. There was no sign of anyone.

So I closed my door, sat at my desk and wondered if I was going crazy.

'Eighty-five minus twenty-eight,' I said, for the third time.

'As I told you,' came the same voice, more

impatiently this time, 'the answer is fifty-seven.'

I leaped out of my seat and looked under my bed and in my wardrobe, before sitting back at my desk in disbelief.

It was then that I saw the hamster peering at me through the bars of his cage.

'It's rude to stare,' he said.

I gasped.

'Not *you*?' I said, astonished.

He looked behind him as if there might be another talking hamster in the cage.

'I *guess* so,' he said.

'You know how to . . . ?'

'Do basic maths?'

'I was going to say "talk".'

'I can hear things too, as it happens,' he snapped. 'Like your family discussing my *you-know-what* over dinner.'

14

'Sorry,' I said, blushing. 'My dad does get a bit overexcited sometimes.'

'And "Jasper Stinkybottom"?' he continued, in the same annoyed tone. 'How would you like it if you were called – I don't know – "Roger Smellington" or "Sebastian Poo-Poo"?'

'Not much,' I admitted. 'Especially not "Sebastian Poo-Poo".'

'But it's done now, I suppose. You may call me "Stinky".'

'OK, "Stinky". I'm Ben.'

'So, Ben – you're not very good at maths, I take it?'

'Or writing. Or science. Or art. Or anything, really.'

There was a silence.

'Fifty-seven,' he said.

'Excuse me?'

'The answer to your question.'

'Oh. Thanks.' I scribbled it down. 'And I need to show the working-out too. Otherwise, Beardy McCreedy will think I used a calculator. He's suspicious like that.'

'Beardy McCreedy?'

'My teacher. He's got this enormous beard. And he hates kids.'

Ten questions, and answers, later, I stuffed the book back into my bag and took out my writing homework: *Describe your house*.

With Stinky's help, it was a piece of cake. He described my room as 'unkempt', which is a fancy way of saying messy, he told me.

'I don't suppose you know any French, do you?' I asked him, fishing out my final bit of homework.

'*Mon français n'est pas mauvais, pour un hamster,*' he said.

'Sorry?'

'I said, "My French isn't bad, for a hamster".'

'Fantastic,' I said.

'*Fantastique,*' he corrected.

Chapter 3

So every day, as soon as I got home from school, instead of watching TV or squabbling with my sister, I'd go straight to my room to do my homework. At first my mum looked at me like I might be ill.

One night though, two weeks after Stinky's arrival, we got home really late. My mum, dad and I had been to see Lucy in a concert after school. It was called 'Funky Monkeys'. All the kids were dressed up as apes of some kind. It was so dull – as boring as being in class with Beardy McCreedy, only with more tap-dancing-related headaches.

The only good part was that we stopped for chips on the way home. My dad said it was a special treat for the whole family, on account of the 'wonderful' costumes (my mum had made them), Lucy's 'brilliant' performance (she was Third Chimp from the Left) and *my* suddenly amazing grades at school (I suspected that the real reason for the treat was that my dad was a very big fan indeed of chips).

As soon as we got home, I hurried to my room, switched on the light and piled my school books next to the hamster cage on the desk.

'Hi, Stinky,' I said, sitting down. 'Maths again. How's your multiplication?' No answer. I peered into the cage and saw him curled up in his little house. 'Stinky?' I said, louder (but not so loud that any of the family would hear

of course). 'Stinky?' My heart was beating like a drum roll now. Maybe he was dead. Maybe I'd killed him with too much homework.

'STIN-KY!'

'For crying out loud!' he snapped. 'I'm trying to sleep here.'

I sighed with relief.

'I thought you were supposed to be nocturnal,' I said. 'You know – awake at night. We did it in science last week. Bats and badgers and things like that.'

'Hamsters,' he said sniffily, 'are actually crepuscular.'

'Crep-what?'

'Crepuscular. Active at dawn or dusk. It's the reason – in case you hadn't noticed –

that I'm usually awake when you're doing your homework. Or when *I'm* doing your homework, I should say.'

'Sorry for waking you up, Stinky,' I said, 'but you're awake now, aren't you?' I clicked my pen and hovered it over my book. 'What's eleven times three?'

He didn't speak.

'Don't you know?' I said, shocked. In the last two weeks, he'd been able to answer every question I'd asked.

'Of course I know,' he grumbled. 'But I'm not giving you the answer. I'm on strike.'

He turned his back to me, showing me his furry bottom.

22

'On strike?'

'I'm not answering any more questions until you help *me* out for a change,' he said, his whiskers twitching.

'What do you need?' I asked him, eyeing my towering pile of homework.

'Number one: clean my place out. So far you have failed to do this even once. This,' he said, jabbing a paw at the newspaper that lined his cage, 'is two weeks old. A *rat* couldn't live in this squalor. How would you like to sleep twenty-two centimetres from your own poo?'

'Not much,' I admitted. 'I'll clean it up tonight. Really.'

'Number two,' he added, 'get me something decent to eat. The food here is terrible. It's *always* grain. *Grain*. Grain, grain, grain. Would you be happy if your parents made the same boring food night after night?'

'They pretty much do,' I told him. But then I had an idea. 'I'll get you some cheese! There's definitely some cheese in the fridge.'

He shook his head.

'Actually hamsters don't like cheese. It upsets our digestion.'

'Upsets your what?'

He sighed impatiently.

'It gives us runny poos,' he said.

'What would you like then?' I asked, quickly changing the subject.

'I thought you'd never ask. Nuts, carrots, lettuce, celery, that type of thing.'

'Great,' I said, springing up out of my chair. 'That's the stuff my mum's always trying to get us to eat. The fridge is full of it. I'll go and get you some now.'

When I came back from the kitchen, I slotted a piece of carrot through the bars of his cage, and he scampered over to it.

'Good carrot,' he said with his mouth full. 'That's good carrot.'

I waited patiently until he swallowed.

'So are you ready for a bit of maths now, Stinky?'

'Number three,' he continued, 'I have a problem with your sister.'

'Join the club,' I said. 'It's her singing, isn't it?'

He shook his head.

'Her dancing?' I said.

'It's worse than that. Today she came in here, reached into the cage and *picked me up*! I don't know if you've ever given any thought to being thrown around by a creature fifty times your size.'

'No, actually.'

'Well, let me tell you, it's not at all fun. Then,' he spluttered, '*then* – she dressed me in a pink tutu from one of her dolls. A *tutu*!'

'I'll deal with her,' I said.

'Promise?'

'Promise.'

'In that case,' he announced, 'the answer to your question is thirty-three.'

'Thanks,' I said, scribbling it down. 'Brilliant.' I smiled at the furry little genius.

'You'll clear out the poo?' he asked.

'Right now. Plus a lifetime's supply of salad is all yours.'

'And you'll definitely take care of your sister?'

I nodded.

But it wasn't my *sister* who started all the trouble.

It was actually my dad.

Chapter 4

'**Y**ou did *what*?' my mum was shouting. 'What on *earth* – what on earth were you thinking?'

Stinky and I were in our room, listening to the argument coming from the kitchen. Luckily (or so it seemed at the time) it was my dad who was in trouble. They'd just got back from parent-teacher night at my school. I'd actually thought they might come back looking pleased, for once.

Apparently not.

'Benjamin Joseph Jinks! COME HERE!'

Now I was really worried. My mum only used my full name when she was completely mad at me. Stinky wished me luck.

My mum was standing with her hands on her hips, and told me to take a seat. I sat down next to Dad at the kitchen table, like we were two naughty kids in the headmistress's office.

And then my mum asked the question:

'Is anybody helping you with your home-work, Ben?'

I took a deep breath. I could hardly explain to my parents that my hamster was, a) able to talk and, b) a genius, could I? They'd think I'd gone bananas. So I said:

'No.'

She gave me that special Mum stare that meant: 'I love you, but if you're lying to me, I'll pull your ears off.'

'Really?' she asked.

'Really,' I answered, and she sighed with relief.

'Because,' she said, glaring at my dad now, 'your father has made a bet.'

Dad looked at me guiltily.

'I was talking to your teacher,' he started. 'Herbert McCreedy. I know him a bit, from running into him now and again at the bookies.' He turned to Mum. 'The man's convinced he can pick winners using some

kind of mathematical formula, which, if you ask me ...'

My mum gave him a withering look.

'Anyway,' my dad continued quickly, 'he told me how amazing

your homework had been recently, and I said, "Great!" and he said, "Well, it would be great, certainly, if he was doing it himself – but he's obviously getting assistance. His homework is flawless – and yet in class he can hardly get an answer right. Having taught mathematics for over thirty years," he said, "I am able to put two and two together." I told him he was wrong. Dead wrong.

He said, "There's a test in two days. If your son fails, and he will, we'll know he's been cheating." That's when I stood up and said: "He'll pass that test –

my boy is lots of things, but he isn't a cheat."
"Want to bet?" he said. "Oh yes," I said. "I certainly do!" And so, er, that was that.'

I sat there, stunned. My mum looked as if her head could explode with rage. I think this might have been even worse than the sticky-tape scenario, except this time it was my dad in trouble. For now. When they found out I'd been cheating, it would be my turn again.

'What was the bet?' I asked.

'You're not going to like it, son,' he said.

'For heaven's sake,' my mum interrupted, 'tell the poor boy.'

'We wrote up a contract,' my dad said sheepishly, handing me a small piece of paper.

I, Herbert Algernon McCreedy, agree to dye my beard bright pink in the (incredibly unlikely) event of Benjamin Joseph Jinks passing his mathematics examination on Wednesday. However, should he fail the test, Benjamin Joseph Jinks will wash my car from top to bottom

I shrugged and looked back at my mum and dad. I wasn't happy, exactly, but it could have been much, much worse. McCreedy's beard was so bushy that you could hide a squirrel in it, so if, by some miracle, I passed the test and he had to dye it pink, it would look absolutely hilarious. On the other hand, washing his car would be annoying, but no big deal. For someone as evil as McCreedy, the forfeit actually seemed quite tame.

'Turn it over,' my mum said. 'There's more.'

I flipped the contract.

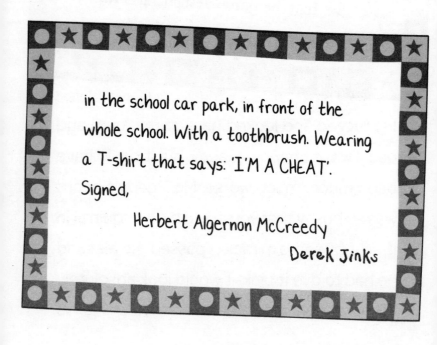

in the school car park, in front of the whole school. With a toothbrush. Wearing a T-shirt that says: 'I'M A CHEAT'. Signed,

Herbert Algernon McCreedy

Derek Jinks

'Oh, *Mum*!' I said.

She looked at me, tight-lipped. 'Don't blame me, blame your father.'

My dad shook his head. 'How about blaming that hairy nincompoop –'

'*Derek!*'

'– who accused our son – our own flesh and blood – of cheating?'

'No, Derek,' my mum said sharply. 'I'd very much prefer to blame you. And how do you know that McCreedy won't cheat and mark all Ben's answers wrong?'

'I thought of that actually,' my dad said, brightening. 'Another teacher is going to check it – someone we can depend on for a fair result.'

This didn't stop my mum from glaring at him for a very long time.

'Now, Ben,' she added, 'you'd better run off to your room and practise your maths, don't you think?'

I got up.

Back in my room, Stinky had been listening, and he must have seen the panicky look on my face.

'Oh dear,' he said.

'What can I do, Stinky? What can I do?'

My hamster always had an answer for everything. But this time, he looked unsure. 'I'll think it over on the wheel,' he announced.

'You'll do what?'

'Jogging on my wheel,' he said, 'helps me to think – and to calm down.'

When he hopped off the wheel a few minutes later, he was really out of breath.

'I have two ideas,' he wheezed.

'Let's hear them then.'

'Number one, you attempt to learn the fundamentals of mathematics in the next forty-eight hours.'

'Hmm,' I said. 'I think you'd better tell me idea number two.'

Chapter 5

The next night – the night before the big test – Stinky and I were going through Plan Number Two one last time.

It was simple. I was going to take him into school in my bag, in an old lunchbox that I'd punched holes in with a fork.

Before the test, when no one was looking, I'd take Stinky out and pop him into my shirt pocket. If I bent my head forward so it looked as if I was thinking really hard, I could whisper the questions to him and just about hear as he whispered the answers back to me.

Now, though, he was pacing up and down his cage.

'You're looking twitchy,' I said.

'I'm a hamster,' he said. 'We're twitchy. We twitch. That's what we do.'

'Twitchier than usual, I mean. You must be nervous about tomorrow.'

'Nervous?' he said. 'Me? Whatever for? Being jiggled up and down in a lunchbox all day? Or being surrounded by hundreds of giant kids?'

He was pretty sarcastic, for a hamster.

But when I thought about what Stinky was going to do for me, I was really grateful to the little ball of fluff. He'd helped me so much, and so I made a big decision. Giving Stinky his freedom seemed like the only way to repay him for all his help, even if it did mean my homework would go back to being rubbish.

'It isn't fair that you're stuck in that cage, Stinky,' I told him. 'So, after tomorrow, I'm going to let you go free. Outside. Forever. I'll miss you, Stinky, and my homework won't be –'

'Are you absolutely insane?' he spluttered. 'Have you lost your mind? Are you completely bananas?' He jabbed one tiny paw towards the window. 'Why would I want to go out *there*?'

'I just thought ... '

'What?'

'You said your cage was like a prison.'

'Have you any idea what my chances are

of surviving even one day outside? Do you know how many types of animal like to eat hamsters?'

I shook my head.

'Practically every single one you can think of. Cats. Dogs. Birds. You name it, they'll be

after me. I leave here, I'm dead meat. A small and fluffy mouthful, I tell you. A furry snack.'

'OK, I get it. Bad idea.'

He went for a run on his wheel. I could tell that he was feeling *really* tense about going to school tomorrow. As he was running, though, I thought of another way to repay him.

When he hopped off, I said, 'OK, then. How about if I go to the pet shop and get you a mate?'

He was out of breath, but managed to wheeze, 'A mate?'

'A mate – you know, a special friend. A girl hamster.'

'Here? In this cage? With me?'

I nodded. He stared at me.

'What do you think?' I asked him.

'I think you want me to die. That's what I think,' he snapped.

'What? Why?' I asked, baffled.

'We're solitary animals. *Solitary*. We like being alone. Put two of us together, and  what you've got on your hands is a fight to the death. Is that what you want? A hamster bloodbath in your bedroom?'

'No,' I said.

He shook his head and went for another run.

Stinky was on his wheel most of the night. Which meant that neither of us got much sleep.

Chapter 6

Even before Ty Hackett strolled over I was feeling shaky. I was sitting on the school field with the lunchbox out in front of me, and Stinky inside it. I reckoned that he needed a bit of fresh air before the test, what with being cooped up in my bag all morning. The holes I'd made in the lunchbox were small, but big enough for air to get in.

Ty Hackett, short for 'Tyson', was this big freckly kid with huge shoulders and a flat nose from being in so many fights. His hobbies included shooting birds with his pellet gun and tying crackling fireworks to the tails of cats. In short, he was no animal lover. So when I saw him walking up to me and Stinky, I got very nervous.

'What you got to eat?' he grunted. 'I'm hungry.'

'Nothing.'

'So what's in there?' he demanded, pointing at the lunchbox.

'It's empty,' I said, but before I could do anything, he stooped and snatched it up.

'Hey, give it back!' I shouted. Ty had this big

evil grin on his face though, and nothing now would stop him from opening it.

But very quickly the smirk was wiped from his face.

He flung the box and howled like when Dad treads barefoot on Lego.

Stinky, somersaulting, tumbled heavily on to the grass.

I jumped to my feet.

Ty Hackett was hopping about crazily.

'It bit me!' he yelled, wide-eyed. 'Your lunch just bit me!'

But I had other things to worry about.

'Stinky!' I called. 'Come back!' But he was scampering across the field, away from Ty Hackett, towards the school building. One moment I could see the grass shaking as Stinky pelted through it, the next he was gone.

Chapter 7

Beardy McCreedy spotted me as I was looking for Stinky in the corridor. The bell had just rung for the end of lunch and the exam was only seconds away.

'Wrong direction, boy!' he boomed at me as I spun round, desperately hunting for my hamster. 'Not trying to escape this test by any chance, are we?'

After Ty Hackett had stomped off, muttering dark threats against me and my furry lunch, I'd searched the entire field and inside the school too, but Stinky was nowhere to be found.

And now McCreedy was marching me into class.

The desks were in single file. I walked to a free one at the back of the room, feeling worried sick about Stinky. Not to mention the exam.

Beardy handed out the tests face down, making sure I was the last. Then he inspected my hands and emptied my pencil case. Finally he looked inside my ears, to make sure I wasn't wearing earphones. Finding nothing suspicious, he barked, 'Begin!'

When I flipped my test paper over, I could hardly bear to look.

And when I did, this was how the exam looked to me:

EXAM

1. Hey! Wasn't the first question supposed to be easy?

2. Without rodent help, Question 2 was also completely impossible. Where was Stinky?

3. What were my chances of passing the test?

    A Incredibly small ☐

    B Zero ☐

    C Absolutely no chance at all ☐

Where on earth had my hamster gone?

I chewed my pen. I scratched my head. I looked around the room.

The clock was ticking. McCreedy had given up staring at me and was now having a sneaky read of the *Racing Post*. All the other kids were concentrating on the questions, except Stuey Jones at the desk nearest the door, who was fidgeting and wriggling in his seat. Then I saw something else move. I had to clamp my mouth shut to stop a gasp escaping.

It's hard to blend in when you're in a maths exam and you're small and furry.

I looked at McCreedy, who was still studying the newspaper. Then I looked around the class again and saw that everyone was still staring at their tests. So I nodded my head to Stinky, to mean, 'Now!'

He darted from the door to the first desk, where Stuey Jones was still fidgeting, his right foot bouncing up and down like it was on a spring. Stinky swerved, only a centimetre from being squashed under a size-eight shoe, and scurried towards me, shimmying around bags and feet, and weaving between table and chair

legs. By the time he skidded to a stop under my desk, both of us were a bit breathless.

I leaned forward to scoop him up, but before my hand reached the floor, McCreedy had leaped out of his chair.

'Boy!' he yelled. 'Benjamin Jinks!' Everyone turned to look at me. 'What on earth are you doing?'

I straightened up.

'I dropped something, sir,' I said.

Which was a very stupid thing to say, because of course everyone in the room turned to look at the floor under my desk.

At first I couldn't bring myself to look. Then, reassured by the blank faces of the other kids, I peeked down.

No hamsters. Nothing.

Phew.

And then everyone went back to what they were doing. Apart from McCreedy, who was still scowling at me suspiciously.

But all I could think was – *Where on earth is Stinky?* One second he was there on the floor, the next he'd vanished. Where could he be?

It wasn't long before I had the answer.

Chapter 8

It started with the faintest of tickles on my sock. Then I felt something creeping under my trouser leg and up my shin and I couldn't help wriggling in my seat. My leg twitched as Stinky edged upwards. The tickly fur made me want to laugh, but the claws, jabbing my skin like tiny needles, made me want to yelp.

When he reached my knee and started edging up my thigh, I was really freaking out. I looked down so McCreedy wouldn't see my face.

I should have been answering Question 5,

but a completely different question was bothering me – just how could Stinky possibly get into my shirt pocket?

And then suddenly he was inside my boxers. I held my breath. It would only take one misplaced paw and...

'Yeeow!' I cried, springing up from my chair like I'd been electrocuted.

The whole class spun around again.

McCreedy's head (or at least the parts not hidden by the huge beard) went a kind of purple.

'Jinks! What now? Do you have ants in your pants?!'

Everyone laughed. Except McCreedy. And me.

Not ants, I thought, and sat back down.

Very. Carefully. Indeed.

'Sorry, sir – pins and needles,' I mumbled.

Everyone giggled.

'Silence!' yelled McCreedy and then gave me a terrifying stare. 'Boy! One more squeak out of you, and it's an automatic fail. And you know what that means.'

I sat there, frozen. At first it seemed as if Stinky couldn't move either. But then he was trying to squeeze up under the elastic waistband of my pants. He pushed and wriggled, kicking his little legs. I sucked my tummy in to help, and he finally squirmed up into my shirt. I was completely exhausted by this time, so I could only guess how Stinky was feeling.

I leaned back in my chair, not out of relief, but so that it would be easier for him to climb straight up my tummy. All this time, Beardy was watching me very suspiciously indeed.

I winced as a paw stabbed into my belly button, and then again seconds later as Stinky negotiated his way past my left nipple. Somehow I managed to stifle a scream.

Stinky was under my collar now.

'Can I come out?' he wheezed, but Beardy's eyes were still fixed on me.

'Not yet,' I muttered through clenched teeth, but just at that moment Stuey Jones knocked a pencil to the floor and McCreedy turned to glare at him. I whispered: 'Now!' and Stinky leaped out and flipped spectacularly into my shirt pocket.

I knew that Stinky deserved a standing

ovation, but instead, I whispered Question 1 to him.

No answer came, so I asked again.

Nothing.

And then, from my pocket, came a very faint sound.

Faint, but unmistakable.

It was the sound of a hamster snoring.

Nothing, not even poking him with a pencil, could wake him.

Stinky stayed asleep until late that evening. He was back in his cage in my bedroom by this time, and I shook my head as he blinked his eyes open.

He shrugged his tiny shoulders. 'I told you I was crepuscular,' he said.

Chapter 9

One week later, after trudging home from school, I went straight to my room, slammed my door and collapsed on to the bed.

'Hey!' Stinky complained. 'Not so noisy! I was having a nap!'

I glared at him as he shuffled out of his little house.

'It's because of one of your naps,' I said, 'that I'm in this mood. Do you know how I spent my lunch break today? I'll tell you how – washing Beardy McCreedy's car. With a toothbrush.  Wearing a T-shirt with "**I'M A CHEAT**" in big letters. With basically the whole school laughing at me.'

'Oh,' he said. 'I see.'

'And,' I added with a sigh, 'McCreedy has a really big car, like the ones that movie stars ride around in.'

My dad knocked on my door and poked his head in. I should have been angry with him, but my dad is one of those people it is hard to be mad at. He'd pull a funny face and you'd forget what the problem was.

'Hello, son,' he said. 'Did I hear someone talking?'

'Only me,' I said. 'I was just talking to myself.'

He frowned, but it was much better for my dad to think I was going a bit nuts than for him to find out about my talking hamster.

 He came into my room, sat next to me on the bed and looked very sheepish.

'How was the you-know-what today?' he asked, making a scrubbing motion with his hand.

'Not good,' I said. 'Pretty bad, in fact.'

'Was it dirty?' he asked. 'The car?'

'There was a lot of bird poo,' I told him. 'I think McCreedy had parked under a tree on purpose.'

My dad grimaced. 'That would not surprise me one bit,' he said. 'There is something quite horrible about that man. I know I shouldn't say things like that about your teacher, but it's true. When I bumped into him the other day and I offered to clean his car instead of you, he wasn't having any of it. He even suggested *another* bet. But I told him "no" of course.'

My eyes widened.

'What was the bet?'

'He said he is so sure you won't pass the *next* test, either, that he'll still dye his beard pink if you pass.'

'And if I fail?'

'You have to wash his car again. Only this time I'll be there too. And I'll be wearing a dress.'

'And you said no?'

'Of course I did. But it's not because I don't think you can do it, son. Or because of the dress. No. This time, I've definitely learned my lesson. Like your mum quite rightly says – no more betting. I feel terrible about what's happened.'

I glanced at Stinky, then looked at my dad and took a deep breath.

'Say yes to the bet, Dad. I'll pass that exam.'

Stinky immediately started running on his wheel. I could tell he was trying to get my attention, but I ignored him.

My dad was frowning at me. 'Really?' he said. 'You really want me to take the bet?'

I nodded, and he stayed quiet for a while. All this time my hamster was racing around on his wheel.

'And you're confident you'll pass?' my dad asked.

I nodded again.

'Because obviously I'd prefer not to be wearing a dress in front of your entire school,' he added. 'I don't really have the figure for it these days.'

'I can do it, Dad.'

'OK then, son,' he said. Then he ruffled my hair and stood up. 'It's probably best we don't tell your mum about this yet,' he added, and left the room with a grin.

Stinky, though, wasn't looking nearly so happy.

Chapter 10

Stinky glared at me through the bars of his cage until my dad was well out of hearing range.

'Have you completely and utterly lost your mind?' he spluttered. 'Because if you so much as think I'll be putting even one paw inside that school of yours again, you must have had a brain explosion. No way. Never. Not on your nelly.' He was looking very agitated indeed. 'Last week,' he added, 'when I went to your school, I nearly died five times. Six, actually, if you count being stuck in your underpants.'

'But I don't want you to come to school, Stinky.'

He stared at me, speechless.

But my hamster never stayed speechless for long.

'Without *me*,' he announced sniffily, 'you have about as much chance of passing a maths examination as a *toad* has of winning a *beauty contest*.'

But suddenly there was a twinkle in his eye.

'Aha,' he said. 'I get it. *Very clever*. You actually *want* to fail, so your dad has to wear a dress. To punish him for making the bet in the first place.'

I shook my head. For possibly the first time, Stinky was completely wrong about something.

'I don't ever want to see my dad in a dress,' I said. 'Plus, if you think I was a laughing stock today when I washed that car, just imagine how it will be if my dad's next to me, wearing my mum's clothes.' I actually shuddered at the thought. 'No, I've learned my lesson, Stinky. What we did before – *you* doing my homework for me, *you* coming into the exam –

that was actual *cheating*. It was wrong. This time, I'm going to pass that test, and I'll do it on my own.'

Stinky let out a groan. 'How very noble,' he said. 'There is, however, a slight flaw in your plan.'

'Oh?'

'Yes – the flaw is that there are probably *worms* with more ability in mathematics than

you, Ben. And *you've* got ten fingers to count on.'

'That's why you're going to teach me.'

Stinky almost choked. 'Me? Teach you?'

'Yes.'

'And why would I want to do that?'

I shrugged. 'Because we're friends? And because there's absolutely nothing better to do here since Mum put all my things in the shed.'

He sighed, and stared at me for what seemed like a minute.

'OK,' he said. 'We'll give it a try. But you have to do *whatever I say*.'

'Yes, sir.'

'Good. And you can start by buzzing off and letting me get some sleep.'

Chapter 11

My first ever maths class with a rodent started badly. I'd rushed home from school and was sitting at my desk with a pencil in my hand, ready, and a little notepad open in front of me. Stinky was out of his cage and sitting beside the pad. He cleared his throat to get my attention.

'To begin with,' he said, 'I want you to clean out my cage.'

I frowned at him. He was supposed to be teaching me multiplication and division. I had a lot to learn, and I certainly didn't have time for chores. There were only two weeks before the next test.

'Really?' I said. 'You want me to –?'

'Clean out the cage,' he snapped.

I groaned. Stinky was my teacher now, and I'd asked him to help me, but all that power must have gone to his head. Maybe he'd turn out to be a smaller but equally hairy version of McCreedy.

I even looked to see if there were any signs of a beard appearing on Stinky's chin before sighing and opening the cage to clean it out.

'First of all,' he said, 'before you do anything, I want you to count all the droppings in there.'

'The what-ings?'

'Droppings,' he repeated impatiently. 'My poos.'

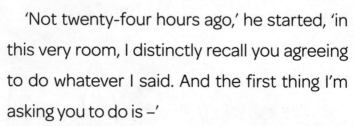

I stared at him in disbelief. 'You're actually asking me to –'

'Not twenty-four hours ago,' he started, 'in this very room, I distinctly recall you agreeing to do whatever I said. And the first thing I'm asking you to do is –'

'OK, OK.'

So I started counting his tiny poos. For such

a small animal, he'd done a
whole lot of them.

'Maybe I feed you too
much,' I muttered. 'You're
like some kind of poo
machine.'

'That,' he said, 'is no way
to talk to your teacher.'

'Teachers don't usually
ask students to count their –'

'Concentrate!' he snapped. So I did.

'There are thirty-nine,' I announced
eventually.

'That's good,' he said. 'Now,
please remove thirteen of
those droppings.'

I picked thirteen out, one by one, and dropped them into an old plastic bag, pulling a face.

'Now, he asked, 'how many droppings are left in the cage?'

I shrugged.

'So, count the remaining ones,' he said, and I did.

'Twenty-six.'

'Take away another thirteen,' Stinky instructed me.

I did, and then he asked me to do it one last time, until there were no hamster droppings left at all.

'Now is it time to start the lesson?' I asked him.

'No,' he said. 'Now it is time to wash your hands.'

When I came back from the bathroom, he said: 'I'm somewhat peckish. All this teaching is making me hungry. I would like some grain, please. Four pieces exactly.' I counted them out and put them on the desk in front of him. He ate them up in no time. 'Actually, I'm rather famished,' he continued. 'Four more grains, if you don't mind.'

'No wonder you poo so much,' I grumbled, and he glared at me.

'Four. More. Grains,' he repeated, and I counted them out.

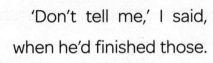

'Don't tell me,' I said, when he'd finished those.

'You'd like four more.'

'If you'd be so kind.'

He gobbled them all up, burped and said: 'Now, write all those sums down.'

I stared at him, blankly. 'What sums?'

'How many droppings were in my cage at the beginning?'

'Thirty-nine.'

'And how many groups of thirteen droppings was that?'

'Three.'

'So write it down,' he said, shuffling onto my pad, and pointing out with a paw what I should do. 'Good,' he said, when I'd finished. 'Now do the grain sum.'

At the end of the lesson, my page looked like this:

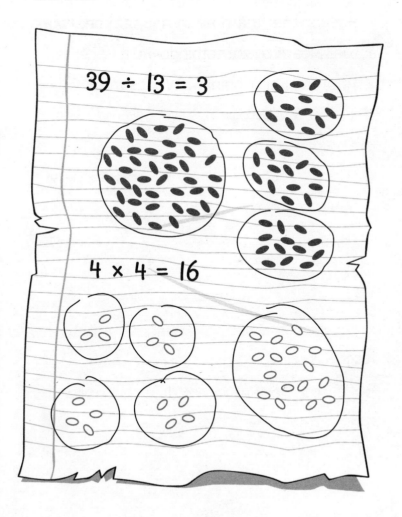

By the time my mum called me for my tea, my brain was exhausted.

But for the first time in a long time, I was actually learning something. And it felt great.

Chapter 12

It was two minutes before the test and I was so nervous I could hardly grip my pencil.

McCreedy had made me sit in the middle of the front row, so he could keep a special eye on me. It's hard to concentrate when someone is staring at you the whole time. And, to make things worse, he'd put me next to Stuey Jones.

Stuey Jones was the biggest fidget in the

class, if not the whole world. He twitched even more than my hamster. No doubt he'd be constantly clicking his pen and tap-tapping his feet the whole exam, or wriggling around in his seat.

McCreedy coughed to get everyone's attention.

'I think you all know,' he started, 'about the bet that I have with Benjamin Jinks's father. And I am hoping this will be a lesson to you: *Cheats never prosper.*' He glared at me as he said those words. My face felt hot.

Then he walked around, handing out all the papers, leaving me till last. 'Begin!' he boomed.

Everyone started scribbling immediately. Apart from Stuey Jones, who was drumming his fingers on the desk. And apart from me. I froze.

I looked down at the questions. They were extremely tricky – even harder than the last test. I glanced up at Beardy and he was staring at me with this big evil grin on his face.

Then I looked back at my test.

People say they have butterflies in their stomach, to mean they're really nervous. But butterflies are nice things, and what I was feeling wasn't nice at all. I had this sick feeling, and my tummy felt completely empty. I could hardly *breathe*, let alone think.

I was trying to concentrate on the test, but all that was in my mind was me and Dad washing Beardy's car, with the entire school surrounding us, pointing and laughing their heads off.

Calm down, I thought. Remember what Stinky said. These aren't numbers on this page. They're grains and poos and I can do this.

So I took a deep breath and started the test. Maybe I wouldn't pass. Maybe I really wasn't clever enough. But one thing was for sure – I'd try my best.

Chapter 13

When I walked into class the next morning, there was a huge buzz of excitement.

This was very strange, because no one had ever got excited about Mr McCreedy's lessons before. Beardy himself wasn't there yet, but the class was full and everyone was chattering and laughing as if it was Christmas.

What was going on?

I sat down, and noticed that everyone was looking at me. Some kids were clapping. Others were cheering.

'What's happened?' I said to Stuey Jones, who was the nearest.

'You mean you haven't heard?' he said excitedly. 'You passed the test!'

I could hardly believe it. An amazing wave of relief washed over me. Kids who usually ignored me came over to pat my back or give

me high-fives. Girls actually smiled at me. Laura Jubb even gave me a hug. It was like a dream, a very strange but brilliant dream.

It got even more amazing though when Beardy McCreedy walked into the room.

There was a moment of complete silence. Even Stuey Jones was still for a second.

And then the whole class erupted into a gigantic roar of laughter, which bounced off the walls and showed no signs of stopping.

McCreedy was scowling. His face had turned a deep shade of purple and his expression was a mix of embarrassment and fury. But his beard was the best bit. It was *bright pink*, like someone had glued candy-floss to the bottom half of his face.

'Silence!' he yelled. 'I will have silence in my class!'

But it would be a very long time before that happened.

A very, very long time indeed.

I was a hero, and I had my incredible hamster to thank.

Stinky was so much better than an aardvark, or a monkey or any of those other pets on that list I'd given to my mum. Yes, he could be grumpy. He was also really bossy and he did smell a bit, sometimes.

But I had to hand it to Stinky: my hamster was definitely a genius.

He was the best pet anyone could ever have.

Look out for the second
STINKY and JINKS
adventure...

A STINKY and JINKS ADVENTURE

MY HAMSTER IS A

SPY

DAVE LOWE

ILLUSTRATED BY
THE BOY FITZ HAMMOND

PICCADILLY
PRESS

Dave Lowe grew up in Dudley in the West Midlands, and now lives in Brisbane, Australia, with his wife and two daughters. He spends his days writing books, drinking lots of tea, and treading on Lego that his daughters have left lying around. Dave's Stinky and Jinks books follow the adventures of a nine-year-old boy called Ben, and Stinky, Ben's genius pet hamster. (When Dave was younger, he had a pet hamster too. Unlike Stinky, however, Dave's hamster didn't often help him with his homework.) Find Dave online at @daveloweauthor or www.davelowebooks.com

Born in York in the late 1970s, **The Boy Fitz Hammond** now lives in Edinburgh with his wife and their two sons. A freelance illustrator for well over a decade, he loves to draw in a variety of styles, allowing him to work on a range of projects across all media. Find him online at www.nbillustration.co.uk/the-boy-fitz-hammond or on Twitter @tbfhDotCom

Thank you for choosing a Piccadilly Press book.

If you would like to know more about our authors, our books or if you'd just like to know what we're up to, you can find us online.

www.piccadillypress.co.uk

You can also find us on:

We hope to see you soon!